DINOSAUR SOUP
(AND OTHER DUBIOUS RECIPES WRITTEN BY CHILDREN)

Illustrations by Mark S Fisher
marksfisher.com

Designed and published by Bob's Your Uncle
25 Channel Center Street, unit 101
Boston, MA 02210 USA
bobsyouruncle.com

Printed by JS McCarthy in Augusta, Maine, USA
This book is printed using soy based inks on paper derived from responsibly
managed forests at a wind powered facility.

ISBN 978-0-9816782-1-4

THANKS

to Abby, Aidan, Alexis, Amelia, Andrew, Angus, Annabelle, Anson, Cameran, Carolynne, Charlotte, Chloe, Chloë, Cooper, Dasha, David, Devon, Duncan, Eleanor, Ethan, Evy, Gracie, Gregory, Isaac, John, Julian, Juliet, Katrin, Keaton, Kelsey, Lena, Lily, Liza, Lucas, Maggie, Malcolm, Matty, Maximus, Mckenzie, Michela, Oliver, Ryann, Ryden, Sandrine, Stacey, Taylor, Todd, and everyone else that contributed recipes to this project, children and parents alike.

INTRODUCTION

You can't make this stuff up.

We sent out a call for submissions to parents to ask their children how
to make their favorite dish, requesting that the child should not be
corrected or advised about any aspect of the recipe, even if measurements,
temperature or timing was way off - that is what we were hoping for!
This book is a collection of our favorites.

One of the first we received was for *Dinosaur Soup* by Ethan, age 3½.
Basically, you need four dinosaurs and you eat it for seven days, which
actually has some logic to it because four dinosaurs would make an awful
lot of soup.

Other recipes defy logic. Dasha's recipe for *Chicken With Cheese* contains
no cheese and Evy's *Pizza* becomes Chinese food. Others are more subtle
with instructions such as "put in the refrigerator for 1 minute," or "cook at
40 degrees for 9 minutes." Many are delightfully vague: "You have to cook it
and that's it." Most of the recipes are not complete until you eat them.

Mark Fisher and I worked together on the ideas for the illustrations that
accompany each recipe. Some were obvious: "a whole live pig" or "a barrel
of strawberries"; others, not so much, as in "bake it for 1,000 hours," which
turns out to be about a month and a half.

Some of the feedback we had along with the submissions told us that the exercise turned out to be great fun as a project for children and adults alike and that it is a great way to occupy and engage with the kids.

We have collected many more and are already working on volume two. If you have a recipe you would like to submit please go to our web site: bobsyouruncle.com.

As Dasha would say, "enjoy!"

Martin Yeeles
Bob's Your Uncle

DISCL

These recipes contain partially cooked, completely uncooked, totally overcooked, and/or readily unavailable or non-existent ingredients. Preparation as directed is not advised and as shown will almost certainly result in inedible meals and food-borne illnesses. Recipes featured are for entertainment purposes only. In short, do not try this at home!

AIMER

RECIPES

BREAKFAST

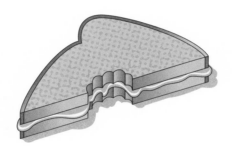

BREAKFAST IN BED FOR MOM & DAD

by ANSON (age 5)

Put cereal into biggest bowl ever and add too much milk. Put Cheese Whiz onto 6 pieces of bread and fold in half. Take upstairs on tray and give cereal to dad and offer a sandwich to your little brother and give mom a half eaten sandwich. Enjoy cuddles in bed afterwards!

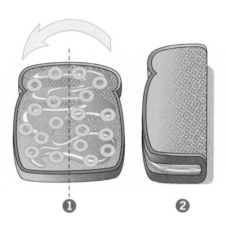

❶　　　　　❷

CHEERIO TACO
by CHARLOTTE (age 4)

Get a piece of bread. Squeeze honey on it.
Then put Cheerios in it. Fold it and then eat it.

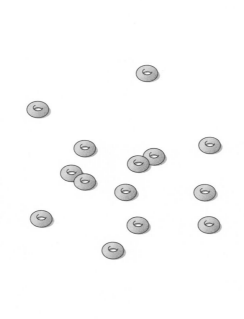

CHEERIOS STRAWS
by AMELIA (age 8)

Take a cheerio. Lick the cheerio. Take another cheerio. Lick that cheerio. Stick the two cheerios together. Carry on with the same thing until you are satisfied with your cheerio straw. Then stick it in a glass of milk and drink through your cheerio straw. Then eat it!

THE WAFFLE JELLY
by LIZA (age 4)

First the waffle. And then the jelly. And then the whipped cream. And then the strawberry on top.

WAFFLES
by ANNABELLE (age almost 4)

You get waffles from the freezer and you cook them. You put cinnamon on them. And you put butter on them. No syrup because I don't like syrup.

TRIPLE BIPPLE MUFFINS
by ALEXIS (age 4)

Chocolate chips
Blueberries
Coloring food

Mix it all together with a hose or a spoon.
And you have to put in some water. That's
why I said hose. Add bananas and paper
strips inside. And flower petals too.

BLUEBERRY MUFFINS

by DEVON (age 4)

Blueberry
Sugar
Dough
Salt

Put into muffin things. Put them in the oven.
Keep them there for a while. Take out. Eat them.

MUFFINS
by MALCOLM (age 4)

Egg
Cinnamon
Chocolate

You put egg in a bowl and cinnamon and chocolate. Bake them.

SOUPS & SALADS

DINOSAUR SOUP
by ETHAN (age 3½)

Take 4 dinosaurs. Put in a bowl. Add some water.
Put in the microwave. Eat it for seven days.

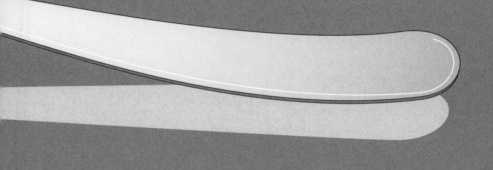

GRAMMY SOUP
by OLIVER (age 3 ½)

Peas
Water
Carrots
Green beans
1 Jumping bean

Cook it and then eat it.

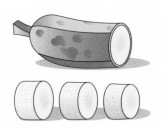

BANANA SOUP
by KEATON (age 6)

Lemonade
Oil
Sugar
Bananas
Water

Take a little bit of lemonade, you pour one amount of sugar, two amounts of oil, 3 amounts of banana into a bowl, and add boiling water. You have to stir it of course.

KELSEY'S FAVORITE SALAD

by KELSEY (age 2½)

Mix with cheese, eggs, and peanuts, then milk and stir. Then play with toys and later put in some monkey juice and salsa. Cook for long and hot. Then I eat it with everybody.

POTATO SALAD

by JULIET (age 6)

6 potatoes
Cheese, cut up in 4 pieces
Some lettuce

Mix it all together.

PASTA & PIZZA

MEATBALLS & SPAGHETTI

by ISAAC (age 4)

You put some stuff that you don't know what it is, it's kind of tricky stuff called like a zacabok or a likaboka and you roll it into circles like your kids like it and then you put it in the oven and when the timer dings it turns out to be meatballs. And it turns out to be meatballs that your kids love and they say, "great mommy!" and every time they do they give you hugs. And then you put them in spaghetti and it's made out of long things that are wiggly, and then your kids will really like them.

And then they will eat it with their meatballs, but some kids don't eat sauce. But sometimes they do, and they put cheese on top of the sauce. Me? I'm not putting sauce on top of mine. But then they say, "I like it mommy!" and then they give you kisses. And then for dessert they might want some sundaes and your mommy makes the greatest sundaes in the world with whipped cream and a cherry on top and in a kid's bowl. And that is the recipe for meatballs and spaghetti.

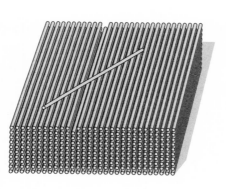

SPAGHETTI

by DAVID (age 10)

Boil the water. Put spaghetti in (300 pieces). Wait for it to be done. Feel it with a fork every once in a while. When its done put it in the draining thing. Put it back in the pot and tell people its time for dinner.

SPAGHETTI
by McKENZIE (age 2½)

Put noodles in a pot. Cook them until they are soft. Put sauce in another pot, cook it until it splatters on the stove. Then mix it together. Put some cheese on it and eat it.

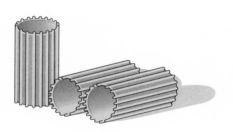

MAC & CHEESE
by CAMERAN (age 4)

You'll need 1 slice of cheese and 100 noodles. Put the noodles and cheese in a pan. Melt the cheese. Put in the oven at 100 degrees for 100 hours. Then take it out and eat!

MAC N' CHEESE
by AMELIA (age 3)

You put milk in it. You have to put the flavoring in it. You put it in the microwave. You stir it. Then you eat it.

RAVIOLI
by ETHAN (age 5)

You get noodles and put them in sauce and cook it and then you get meatballs and put it in and that's how you make it and then you put it in a bowl and get a spoon and then sit at the table, take your shirt off so you don't ruin it and then you eat it!

MAKING A PIZZA
by EVY (age 2)

You use bread and some tomatoes and onions and mushrooms. Then you you put cheese on it and put some pasta on it, and chicken. And you cook it and you make into Chinese food.

DINNER

SPINACH & POTATOES
by LUCAS (age 6)

Spinach
Potatoes

You put spinach and potatoes in the pot and then you cook them together and you stir them around a few times, then you cook them once more. Then you keep looking in there to see if its done and then one more time you stir it around.

CHICKEN NUGGETS
by ABBY (age 5)

You find the bag and put them in the microwave. You push a button on the microwave. You push number three. Then you wait until it's done. Then you wait until three minutes. And then for lunch I will have Macaroni and Cheese.

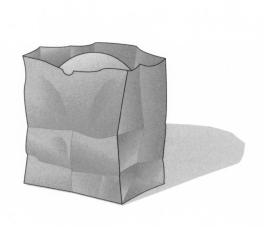

THANKSGIVING TURKEY

by CHLOE (age 5)

Get a turkey at the store. Cook it at your house. Cook it for 10 minutes. Get it out of the oven. Put a little bit of salt on it. Eat the turkey and dip it in barbeque sauce.

CHICKEN WITH CHEESE
by DASHA (age 5)

Put chicken in the oven for 5 minutes. Then put ketchup on chicken. Enjoy.

BLT
by COOPER (age 8)

You get the good bread from the bakery
and ask them to slice it. You get the good
tomatoes - Dad said they aren't easy to find
in Vermont in the winter, and some lettuce.
Put them on the bread with a whole, live pig.

HOT DOGS
by CHLOË (age 6)

A bun and a weenie dog

First, you get out the buns. Next, you cook the dogs. Put them in the oven on HOT. That's why they're called HOT dogs. Then when the dogs are done, you put 'em in the buns and then you eat it! That's how you make a hot dog.

MEATBALLS

by LILY (age 5)

First you buy that squiggly red stuff you don't let me touch, put it in your red bowl, crack an egg but try really hard not to get any shells in there, cause it's gross if you pick it out with your fingers, shake those spices you use but only one time or else they will taste spicy. Cut up one of those things that make your eyes watery, oh yeah, an onion, but be careful not to hurt your finger on the knife because then you would have to run upstairs and get a band aid. Put a handful in your silver meatball maker and squeeze in a pan, you can't use the blue one because that's my mom's favorite and she won't let anyone else use it, she doesn't want it ruined. If you break her pan she would probably cry. Ask for help putting them in the magic oven, kids aren't suppose to go near it.

Cook at 40 degrees for 9 minutes.

HAMBURGER
by KATRIN (age 8)

Take a burger. Cook it in a dish for 3 minutes.
Put things on it (mustard, ketchup, cheese).
Eat in a bun.

DESSERT

CHOCOLATE BANANA MASH
by RYDEN (age 3)

Put chocolate chips & smushed up bananas
in a dish. Put on bread & drink with milk,
mommy and a story!

CHOCOLATE & VANILLA ICE CREAM

by RYANN (age 5)

Go to the ice cream store. Order a cone. Tell them to put two spoons of ice cream in the cone. One spoon has chocolate. One spoon has vanilla. Tell your mommy to pay for the ice cream. Eat it!

SPECIAL STRAWBERRY PIE
by TAYLOR (age 4)

Get a barrel full of strawberries. Then you get a bowl and put chocolate in it, you can put as much chocolate as you want. Then a tiny spoonful of wheat flour. Then you bake it, put some strawberries on the top. Cool off and it's ready to go!

JAM TARTS

by ELEANOR (age almost 5)

Wash your hands and squish the pastry in a bowl. Get lumps of pastry (with your hands is best) and roll and roll and roll with a roller. Put jam in the middle and spread it with a spoon. Put in the oven for cooking.

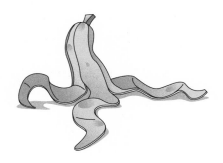

BANANA BREAD
by DEVON (age 4)

Eggs
Sugar
Bananas
Salt
Dough

Put in bread maker. That's all.

BANANA BREAD
by JOHN and MAGGIE (both age 4)

Bananas
Plain eggs
Some flour
Some sugar
Salt
The other stuff we can't measure out with those little spoons

Mash it. Stir it. Put it in the microwave and cook it for one hour.

PUMPKIN BREAD
by ANDREW (age 4 ½)

3 cups of cinnamon
1 cup of pepper
1 cup of salt
2 cups of pumpkin bread
1 cup of olive oil

You have to cook it and that's it.

CAKE

by EVY (age 2)

You mix cake, and spill it, and put frosting on it like a snow man.

CAKE
by STACEY (age 4)

Eggs
Milk
Food coloring

You bake it.

BAKING A CAKE
by MATTY (age 4)

You use use some cake mix, and some eggs, and some butters, and that's all. Then you use a mixer and mix it and put it in the oven to bake it for 1,000 hours. Then you put sprinkles on it and you go to a party.

ORANGE CAKE
by SANDRINE (age 7)

8 tablespoons of flour
1 cup of water
a bit of orange juice
½ cup of milk
9 tablespoons of sugar

Mix with ½ a cup more water. Put in the oven for 2 minutes at 10 degrees.

Icing:
10 liters of white cream
3 tablespoons of sugar

Mix and spread on the cake. Eat the cake.

CHOCOLATE CAKE
by DUNCAN (age 7)

Flour
Eggs
Batch of melted chocolate
Sugar

Pour chocolate batter into bowl. Mix up with the whizzy machine to get the chunks out. Pour into cake shape. Bake it for 20 minutes then take it out of the bowl. Add icing then serve, otherwise eat it.

STRAWBERRY CAKE
by CAROLYNNE (age 4)

3 cups of flour
4 eggs
3 cups of oil
5 teaspoons of salt
Icing:
1 strawberry and sprinkles

Cook in the oven for 7 hours at 49 degrees.

BIG CUPCAKES
by TODD (age 6)

First you make some dough. Add half a cup of milk, then half a cup of sugar. Put in the refrigerator for 1 minute. Take it out and you put in 1 cup of salt. Stir real good. Cook for 8 minutes and then its ready.

LITTLE CUPCAKES
by ANGUS (age 2)

Get some flour and some butter and some sugar and some other sugar and some tomato. Just in a big bowl. And then in the oven. I have to use a spoon and stir it around.

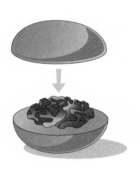

RAISIN STUFFED GRAPE

by JULIAN (age 5)

Take a grape. Cut it in half. Stuff a raisin into one of the halves. Put the grape back together and you've got a raisin stuffed grape.

PURPLE JELLO
by AIDAN (age 3)

Put purple jello stuff into a bowl. Add the thing that makes it jiggle. Add apple juice inside. Put it in the fridge to bake. Wait. Eat it when it's ready.

CHEESE
by LENA (age 6)

Milk from a cow.
Butter
Flour

First put flour in and add some eggs. Then add milk and stir it up. Bake it and shape it like cheese. Put it in wrappers for people to buy at the store. And leave some for us too.

COOKIES

WHOPPER CAKE COOKIES
by MAXIMUS (age 2)

Put in milk. Then put in chocolate milk.
Put in one sippie cup of sugar. Put in 2 eggs.
Then cook the eggs. Then put in a Whopper
Cake. Then make it into a circle.

SUGAR COOKIES
by MICHELA (age 8)

Get a half a bowl of sugar and a half a bowl of salt. Add two eggs. Mix them all together. Don't forget the flour. Put in the refrigerator for 8 minutes, take out and roll in balls and roll in sugar. Put in the oven at 8 degrees and don't let them burn or you'll be sorry.

MARSHMALLOW CHOCOLATE COVERED COOKIES
by GREGORY (age 6)

3 marshmallows
Some chocolate
2 gallons of sugar

First take the marshmallows and mush them all together. Take some chocolate and cover it with 2 gallons of sugar and put them in the freezer. After you bake them put them in the freezer and take them out and cover them and eat them all up. You can decorate them.

CHOCOLATE CHIP COOKIES
by GRACIE (age 3)

Cookie dough
Yellow
Little chocolates

Put the chocolates in and bake it in the oven and in 30 more minutes it's done. So then we get chocolate chip cookies.

HOW TO MAKE:

_____

_____

_____

_____

_____

_____

_____

_____

_____

_____

_____

This recipe is by: _____ Age: _____

HOW TO MAKE:

_____

_____

_____

_____

_____

_____

_____

_____

_____

_____

_____

This recipe is by: _____ Age: _____

BOB'S YOUR UNCLE is a Boston, Massachusetts based company founded by husband and wife Martin and Michele Yeeles in 2001. Originally from England, they moved to the States in 1993 "just for a year or two" and have been in Boston ever since. Martin is a graphic designer, Michele a former shoe designer. "Bob's your uncle" is a British expression used to indicate that a given task is very simple. Possibly inspired by Victorian Prime Minister, Robert Cecil, who appointed his nephew to a ministerial post, therefore to have Bob as your uncle was a guarantee of success.

MARK S FISHER was trained in the commercial arts at various institutions of higher learning in upstate New York, He established his illustration business in the Boston area, circa 1972. His work has garnered recognition from *The Society of Illustrators*, *American Illustration*, as well as *Print* and *Idea* magazines. In addition to Illustrating he indulges in his long passion of making comics, and sculptures out of junk. Visit his web site at marksfisher.com.